The Tale of the Oki Islands

A TALE FROM JA

Retold by Suzanne I. Barchers
Illustrated by Hiromitsu Yokota

RED CHAIR
•PRESS•

Please visit our website at **www.redchairpress.com**.
Find a free catalog of all our high-quality products for young readers.

 For a free activity page for this story, go to
www.redchairpress.com and look for Free Activities.

The Tale of the Oki Islands

Publisher's Cataloging-In-Publication Data
(Prepared by The Donohue Group, Inc.)

Barchers, Suzanne I.
The tale of the Oki Islands : a tale from Japan / retold by Suzanne I. Barchers ;
illustrated by Hiromitsu Yokota.
p. : col. ill. ; cm. -- (Tales of honor)
Summary: When her father is banished by the emperor, Toyoko, a skilled diver, bravely goes
in search of him. In the process, she breaks an evil spell cast on the emperor. Includes special
educational sections: Words to know, What do you think?, and About Japan.
Interest age level: 006-010.
ISBN: 978-1-937529-78-9 (lib. binding/hardcover)
ISBN: 978-1-937529-62-8 (pbk.)
ISBN: 978-1-936163-94-6 (eBook)
1. Courage--Juvenile fiction. 2. Devotion--Juvenile fiction. 3. Fathers and daughters--Juvenile
fiction. 4. Emperors--Juvenile fiction. 5. Folklore--Japan. 6. Courage--Fiction. 7. Love--Fiction.
8. Fathers and daughters--Fiction. 9. Kings, queens, rulers, etc.--Fiction. 10. Folklore--Japan. I.
Yokota, Hiromitsu. II. Title.

PZ8.1.B37 Ta 2013

398.2/73/0952   2012951564

This series first published by:
Red Chair Press LLC   PO Box 333   South Egremont, MA 01258-0333

Printed in the United States of America

1 2 3 4 5 18 17 16 15 14

Once there was a samurai named Oribe, a great
and noble soldier. Oribe served his emperor
faithfully. Sadly, the emperor suffered from
poor health. During one spell of discomfort, he
became very angry with Oribe. The emperor
banished Oribe to the distant Oki Islands.

Now, Oribe loved his daughter more than anything. When Tokoyo was young, he had taught her to dive for oysters. She could hold her breath for a very long time. And she was strong and courageous. Every day he wondered what Tokoyo was doing. And every day she missed her father dearly.

One day, Tokoyo decided she had to find her father. She sold her belongings and walked to a village across the sea from the islands.

She met a fisherman, asking, "Will you take me to the Oki Islands? I'm looking for my father."

The fisherman turned her down. "I am sorry. Haven't you heard the stories? That island is surely cursed." One after another, fishermen refused her request to take her to the islands.

Tokoyo had no choice. That night she stole down to the water's edge in the darkness. She cut loose a small sailboat. All through the night and the next day she sailed across the sea. Once at the island, she fell on the sand, where she slept through the night.

The next morning she began to ask about her father. The first person gave her some advice. He said, "You must be very careful. Strange things happen here. You don't want to anger the gods—or the emperor."

So Tokoyo wandered from village to village, listening to people's conversations. She hoped to overhear something useful. But no one spoke of her father.

One day, she came to a shrine on a rocky cliff over the sea. She prayed for help and dozed off. Soon she awoke to the sound of weeping. Rising, she saw that the cries came from a young girl. The girl was about to be thrown off the cliffs and into the sea.

"Stop!" she called. "What are you doing? And why?"

The startled priest answered. "It is the time of the sacrifice. The Oki Islands are ruled by an evil sea god. He demands the sacrifice of a young girl every year. If we disobey, he sends storms that kill many of our fishermen. We sacrifice one to save many."

"Please let me take her place," Tokoyo begged. "I came to find my father who was banished by the emperor. My life is empty without him. If you will find him and tell him that I love him, I can die in peace."

Tokoyo put on the white robe while praying for courage. She placed a jeweled dagger, her last possession, in her sash. She bowed low to the girl and the priest. Then she dived into the sea.

Tokoyo swam deeper and deeper. At the
bottom of the sea, she saw a huge cave covered
with glittering coral. She took her dagger in her
hand and swam forward. She stopped when
she spied a statue of the emperor near the cave.
Working swiftly, she removed it and swam
back toward the entrance of the cave.

Suddenly, Tokoyo spotted a huge beast wallowing in the heavy sea. Having the advantage of speed and surprise, she swam forward. Tokoyo thrust her dagger into one of its red eyes. As it floundered, she pulled out the dagger and stabbed it in the heart.

The beast drifted to the sea floor, dead. With her last breath, Tokoyo dragged the monster by its arms up through the sea.

The priest and girl rushed down from the cliffs to help Tokoyo drag it onto the sand. "Do you realize what you have done?" the priest cried. "This is the evil sea god. You have broken the spell on our island! We must send word to the emperor at once!"

The emperor sent for Tokoyo. When she arrived, she presented him with the statue and told him her story. The emperor praised her courage.

"You have done me a great service, Tokoyo," said the emperor. "This sea god had cursed me, causing my poor health. You have broken that spell. And now I would like to do something for you. There must be a wish that I can grant."

"There is only one thing I desire," said Tokoyo.
"I wish to have my father, Oribe Shima, home
once again."

"Done!" said the emperor.

From that day forward, Tokoyo and her father treasured their time together. And the people of the Oki Islands never forgot Tokoyo's bravery. In truth, if you go there today, the fishermen and women will probably tell you all about her.

banished: sent away from a place as a form of punishment

emperor: a ruler with great power and rank

sacrifice: to give up an animal or person as an act of honor to God or divine figures

wallowing: rolling lazily or lying about in mud or water

Question 1: Why did the emperor send Tokoyo's father Oribe away to a remote island?

Question 2: Why did the fishermen refuse to take Tokoyo to the Oki Islands in their boats? How did she get there?

Question 3: Describe how you think Tokoyo acted when she saved the young girl from being sacrificed to the sea.

Question 4: How did Tokoyo break the curse on the emperor? Why do you think the people of the island thought there was an evil sea god?

About Japan

Japan's written history dates to the 1st Century AD. Our story dates from the feudal period (1185-1868) and probably from the early 1300s. The samurai, or warriors, rose to power during this time. Samurai ruled over certain lands and peasants for the emperor. If a samurai broke the code of honor, or bushido, he may have been sent away to live alone. The Oki Islands are small isolated islands and the legend of the samurai's daughter is still told there today.

About the Author

After fifteen years as a teacher, Suzanne Barchers began a career in writing and publishing. She has written over 100 children's books, two college textbooks, and more than 20 reader's theater and teacher resource books. She previously held editorial roles at Weekly Reader and LeapFrog and is on the PBS Kids Media Advisory Board. Suzanne also plays the flute professionally – and for fun – from her home in Stanford, CA.

About the Illustrator

Hiromitsu Yokota earned his fine arts degree from Musashino Art University in Tokyo, Japan. His subtle digital illustrations have the appearance of traditional hand-drawn pastels. His artwork is meant to convey 'happiness, here and now.'